THIS BOOK BELONGS
TO

children's
choice®

THE
SNOWY
DAY

To Tick, John, and Rosalie

EZRA JACK KEATS

THE
SNOWY
DAY

Awarded the 1963 Caldecott Medal
for the Most Distinguished Picture Book of the Year

New York · The Viking Press

One winter morning Peter woke up and looked out the window. Snow had fallen during the night. It covered everything as far as he could see.

After breakfast he put on his snowsuit and ran outside. The snow was piled up very high along the street to make a path for walking.

Crunch, crunch, crunch, his feet sank into the snow.
He walked with his toes pointing out, like this:

He walked with his toes
pointing in, like that:

Then he dragged his feet s-l-o-w-l-y
to make tracks.

And he found something sticking out
of the snow that made a new track.

It was a stick

— a stick that was just right for
smacking a snow-covered tree.

Down fell the snow —
plop!
— on top of Peter's head.

He thought it would be fun to join the big boys in their snowball fight, but he knew he wasn't old enough — not yet.

So he made a smiling snowman,

and he made angels.

He pretended
he was a mountain-climber.
He climbed up
a great big tall
heaping mountain of snow —

and slid all the way down.

He picked up a handful of snow — and another,
and still another. He packed it round and firm and
put the snowball in his pocket for tomorrow. Then
he went into his warm house.

He told his mother all about his adventures
while she took off his wet socks.

And he thought and thought
and thought about them.

Before he got into bed he looked in his pocket.

His pocket was empty. The snowball wasn't there.

He felt very sad.

While he slept, he dreamed that the sun
had melted all the snow away.

But when he woke up his dream was gone.

The snow was still everywhere.

New snow was falling!

After breakfast he called to his
friend from across the hall, and
they went out together into the
deep, deep snow.